TOWN MOUSE HOUSE

To our children, Poppy and Harry, and to
Jake, our dog (for his patience) —N.B. & A.H.

TOWN MOUSE HOUSE

How we lived one hundred years ago

Nigel Brooks &
Abigail Horner

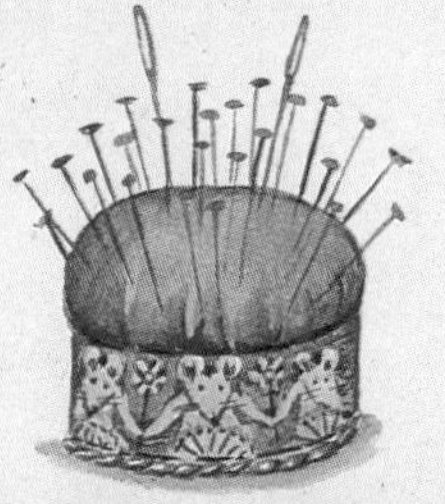

Walker & Company
New York

Welcome

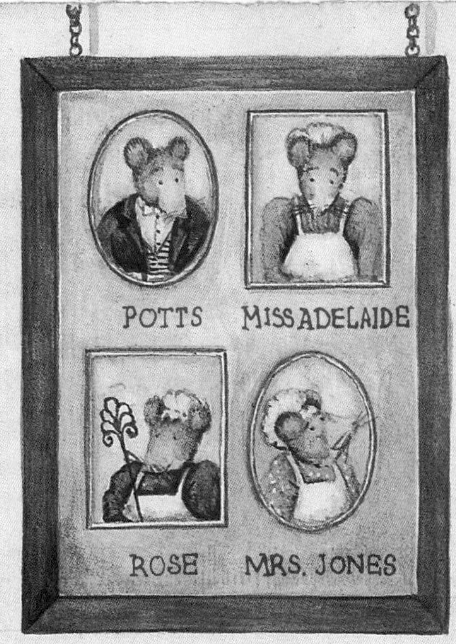

My name is Augustus John Town Mouse. I'd like to show you around our house. I live here with my family: Mama, Papa, and sister, Kate, and baby brother, Gregory; and Potts, the butler, Mrs. Jones, the cook, our nanny, kind Miss Adelaide, and Rose, the parlor maid.

The year is 1900. Come inside . . .

Good morning

In the early morning, when we are still cozy in our beds, the servants are already up and hard at work.

Rose brings us up a tray of tea and toast, then runs downstairs to empty our chamber pots in the bathroom at the end of the hall (she doesn't like this job at all!).

Potts opens the curtains to let in the sun, while down in the kitchen Mrs. Jones plans her recipes for the day. Rose cleans out the grates and then lights the fires, sighing, "A parlor maid's work is never done!"

Doors

Our Front Door

Potts, the butler, is in charge of our big front door. When the bell rings he comes hurrying from the hall. Visitors for Mama and Papa leave calling cards. The postman brings our letters and parcels. I'm waiting for a parcel from my Uncle Teddy in Boston.

Our Back Door

THE DRESSMAKER

THE GROCER

THE CHIMNEY SWEEP

THE COALMAN

THE BAKER'S BOY

THE MILKMAN

Our back door is called the tradesmen's entrance. The doorbell never stops ringing. It's here the servants go in and out. And all day long the tradespeople bring the things we need to keep our big house running smoothly.

Our clothes

Woolly drawers that button down
Collars and cuffs that come off to wash
Boots and shoes and caps and hats
Smart tweed suit for around the town
Handkerchiefs and silk necktie
My favorite sailor suit and hat

Muslin bloomers and camisole
Stockings, gloves, and cotton smock
Drawstring purse and party frock
For summer a pink parasol
A warm wool coat for wintertime
A sailor suit that matches mine

The schoolroom

We don't go out to school. Our governess, Miss Algebra, comes every morning at eight o'clock. We must be good, we mustn't fight, and if we can't get our sums all right and recite our capital cities one by one, she might rap our knuckles with a ruler.

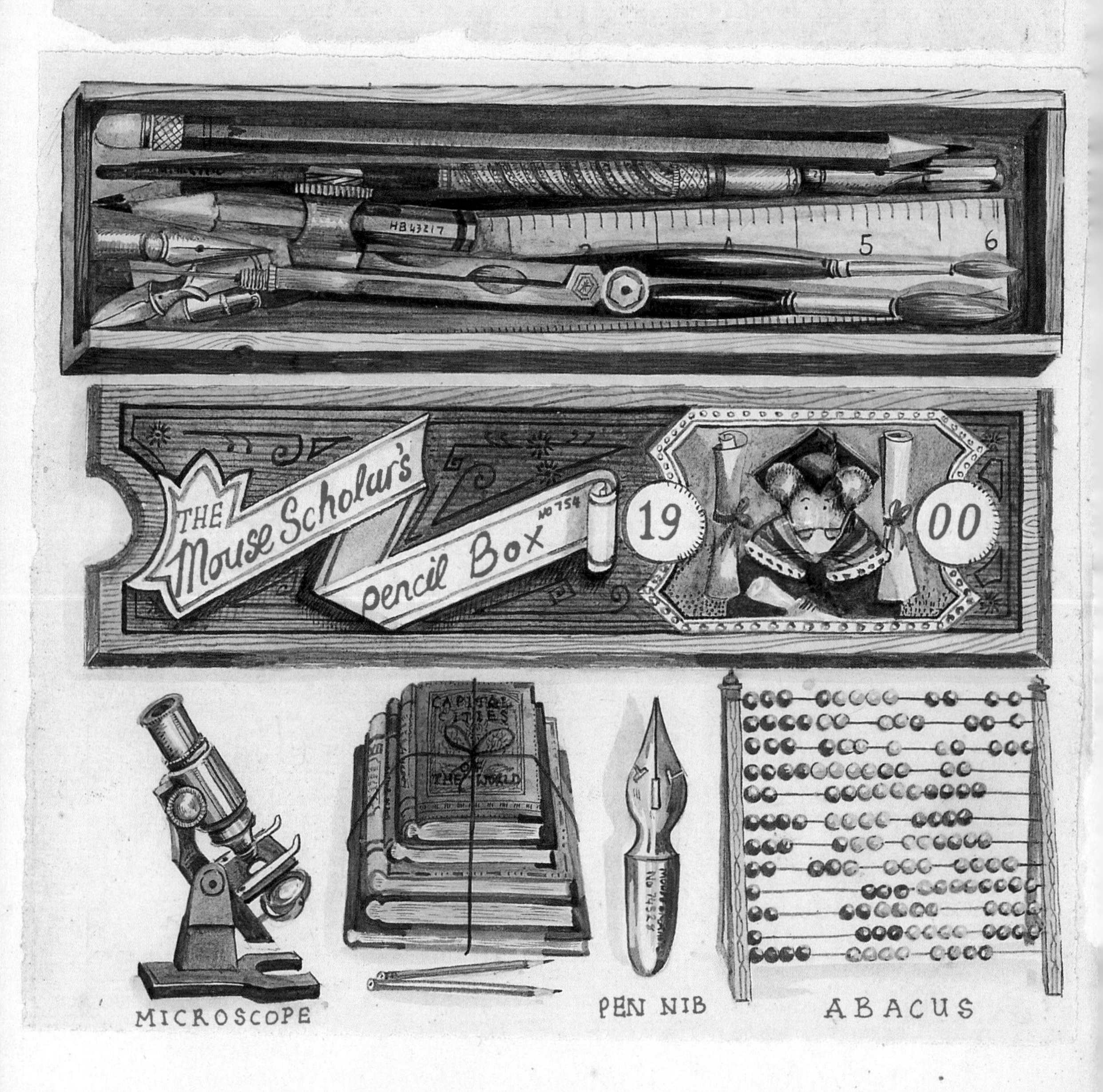

A a B b C c

Mama's dressing room

Getting ready's such a fuss
Mirror, brush, and powder puff
Bottles filled with sweet perfume
Diamond rings and ivory comb
Petticoats and underskirts
Corset pulled so tight it hurts

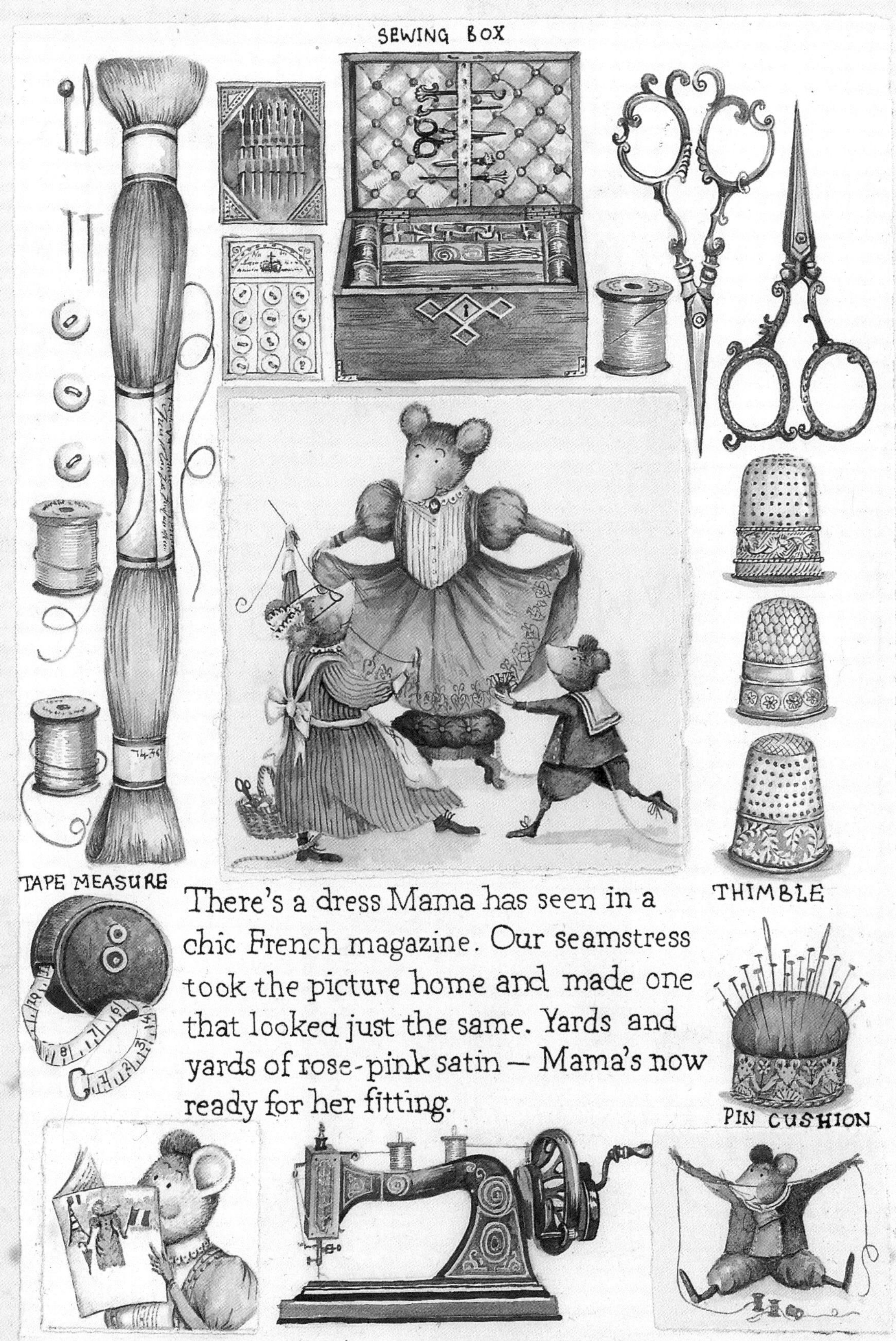

There's a dress Mama has seen in a chic French magazine. Our seamstress took the picture home and made one that looked just the same. Yards and yards of rose-pink satin — Mama's now ready for her fitting.

Papa's study

The study is Papa's private place and he hates to be disturbed. He reads the newspapers, writes his letters, and checks his accounts. Sometimes, though, we are allowed inside and he tells us stories of his adventures as a captain in the navy.

When I grow up I'll be a sailor too and sail the seven seas.

PAPA'S SHIP THE BLACK MOUSE
CAST-IRON CLOCK
WRITING DESK
BIG BRASS TELESCOPE

The town square

The park is across our busy
road where trams rattle
up and down all day.

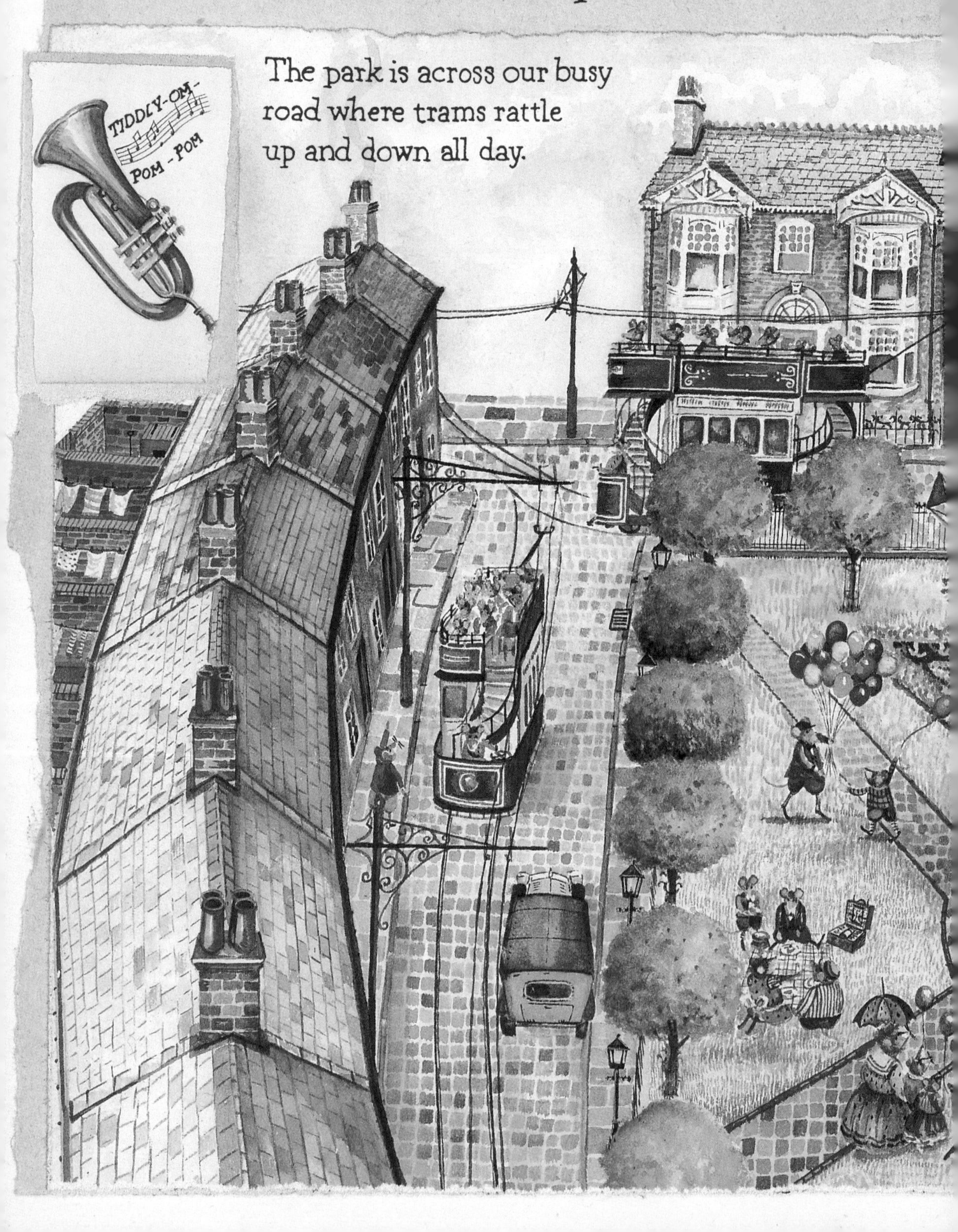

There are flowers and trees and a big bandstand. In summer we go for an afternoon stroll. Nanny pushes Gregory in his pram and when no one's looking holds hands with her young man.

The nursery

Although Kate and I are no longer babies, our playroom is still called the nursery. A rocking horse, a spinning top, china dolls, a ball and cup, a funny tin mouse bank, and Kate's dollhouse with miniature furniture.

My toy train that rattles around and around the track, a clockwork ship with big brass key. Our tin soldiers fight famous battles—blue for Kate and red for me.

Cook in her kitchen

Our cook, Mrs. Jones, is the queen of the kitchen with loads of pots and pans at her command.

With Rose to help, she cooks for everyone. Sometimes (she says) she wishes she had twenty pairs of hands. We love to help her make the dough for her puddings and pies, but most of all the cakes so we can lick the sticky spoon.

All the servants eat downstairs—their breakfast, lunch, tea, and supper. Here Potts pours the wine into a crystal pitcher to serve upstairs, and polishes the silver.

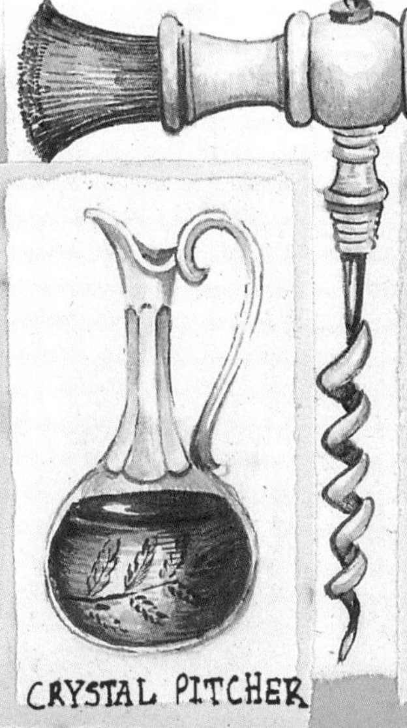

POTTS POLISHES THE SILVER

MRS. JONES PUTS ROSES MADE FROM ICING ON TOP OF HER CAKE

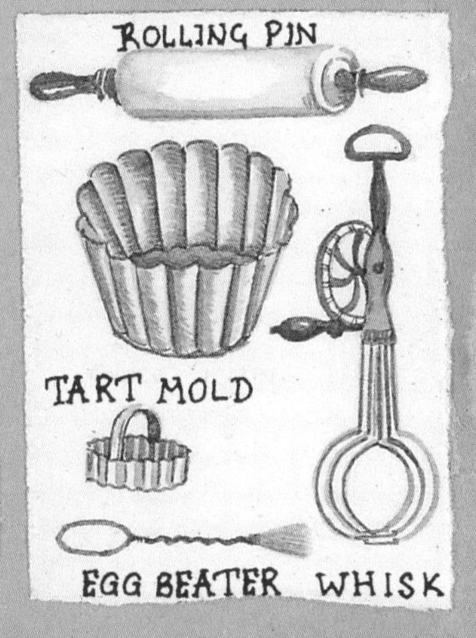

MECHANICAL FRUIT PEELER

ROSE SHINES THE TABLE KNIVES WITH A MACHINE CALLED THE SERVANT'S FRIEND

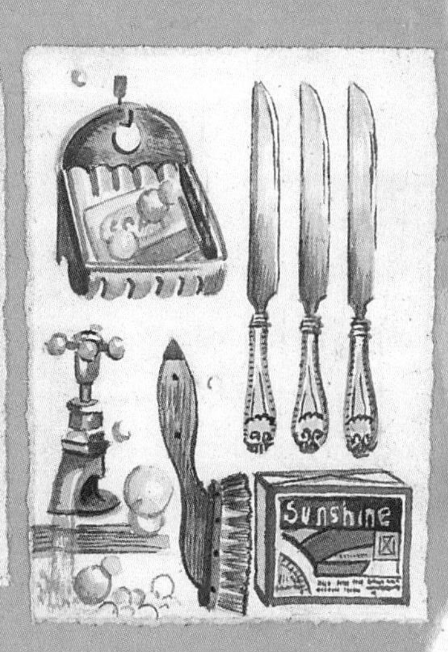

Dinnertime

We eat with Nanny upstairs in the nursery.

On Fridays fish is always served (it's good for us, says Nan). Tonight Mama and Papa have important visitors and downstairs they are served from silver dishes and eat from porcelain plates: roast beef and creamed potatoes and afterward pudding and great big cakes. When we're grown up Mama says we can sit at the table too, but that seems like a long, long time to wait!

LADY BROWN MOUSE
DOCTOR HENRY JOLLY-TAIL
MAMA
MRS. JOLLY-TAIL
THE HONORABLE WILBERFORCE WHISKERS

JOLLY JELLIES

Entertainment

BILLIARDS WITH PAPA

MAMA AND PAPA PLAY WHIST

Sometimes Mama and Papa hold a ball. We're not allowed downstairs, but we creep out to the hall and hope we won't be seen. Secretly, we listen to the grown-ups talk, and watch the dancing.

At the end of the day, if we are all at home and no one's visiting, we sometimes have a game of cards or snakes and ladders, or billiards (which Papa is teaching me to play).

PUZZLES AND QUIZZES IN FRONT OF A ROARING FIRE

Bath-time

Rub a dub dub
Two mice in a tub

Our bathroom has a cast-iron tub. Nanny gives our backs a scrub and washes behind our ears. Papa shaves with foam and brush. Mama is always in a rush. We have an amazing new toilet—quite the latest thing—with a porcelain cistern and a chain to pull to make it flush. In the morning there's often a line, so we really need another one—or two.

Bedtime

Before I lay me down to sleep
I pray the Lord my soul to keep

When we've undressed and said our prayers,
Nanny tucks us into bed and reads to us by gaslight:
stories of ghosts and long lost treasure chests or tales from
the mummy's tomb. We like the scary stories best.

Mama and Papa won't go to bed for hours,
but I know that after midnight when we are
fast asleep, into our room our mama tiptoes
and whispers, "Good night, my little ones."

NIGHTDRESS
HOT MILKY DRINKS
HOT WATER BOTTLE
Mouse Tails of SPOOKY HORROR
PAJAMAS

First published in the United Kingdom in 1999
by Hutchinson Children's Books, Random House UK Limited.
First published in the United States of America in 2000
by Walker Publishing Company, Inc.

Library of Congress Cataloging-in-Publication Data available upon request

ISBN 0-8027-8732-0

Printed in Singapore
2 4 6 8 10 9 7 5 3 1